Usborne

100 Paper Spaceships
to fold & fly

Illustrated by Andy Tudor

Designed by Hannah Ahmed
and Brian Voakes

Turn over for tips on folding,
flying and storing
your paper spaceships.

Useful tips

Here are some helpful tips that will make your spaceships fly more effectively and keep them in good shape.

How to launch your paper spaceship

Here are the best steps to a perfect take-off and landing:

- Stand facing forward.

- Hold each spaceship just in front of its midpoint.

- Pull back and then throw forward in a long, smooth movement to release your spaceship.

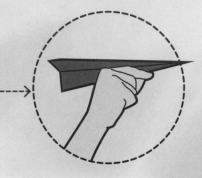

Folding

- Use a ruler to line up the folds and keep them sharp.

- If you want to keep your spaceship for another day, store it flat inside a book.

- If your spaceship gets wet, or won't fly... fold a new one!

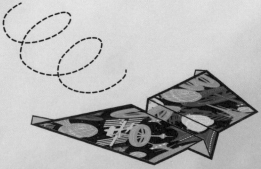

Flying

- Try changing the angle of your spaceship's wings to alter its flight.

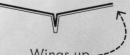

Wings up

Wings down

Add a wing tip fold.

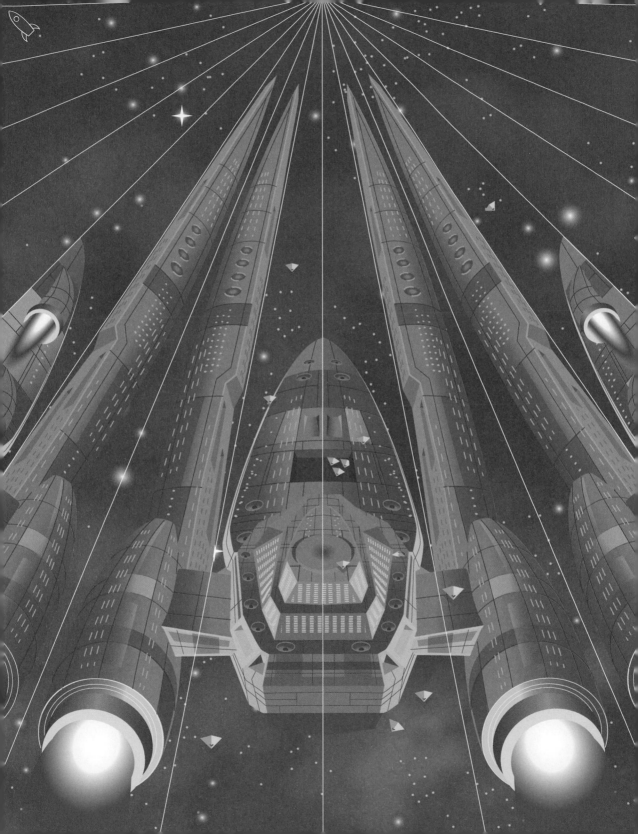

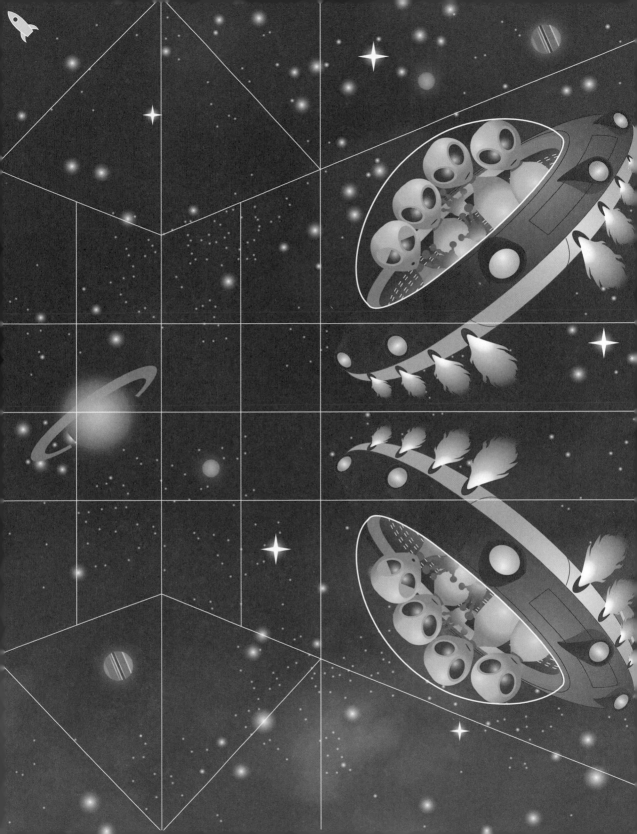

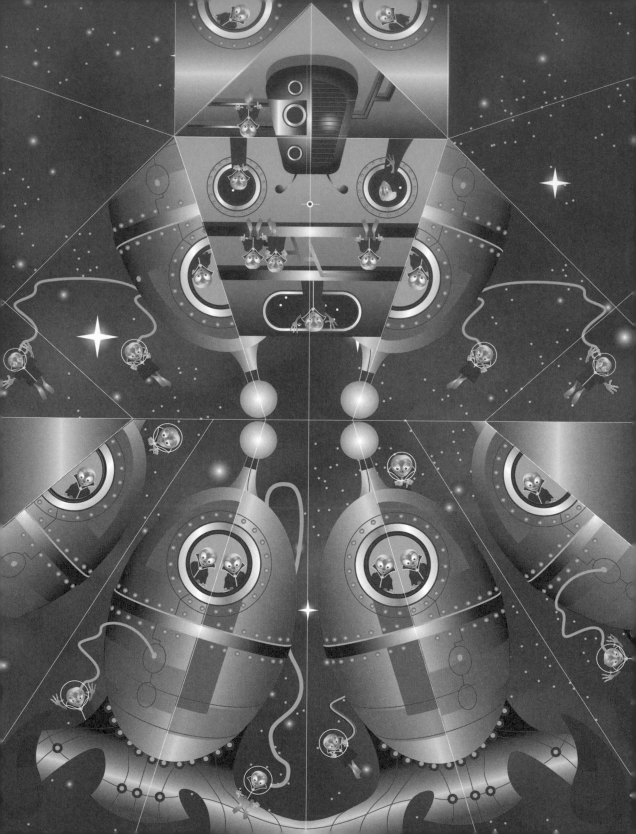

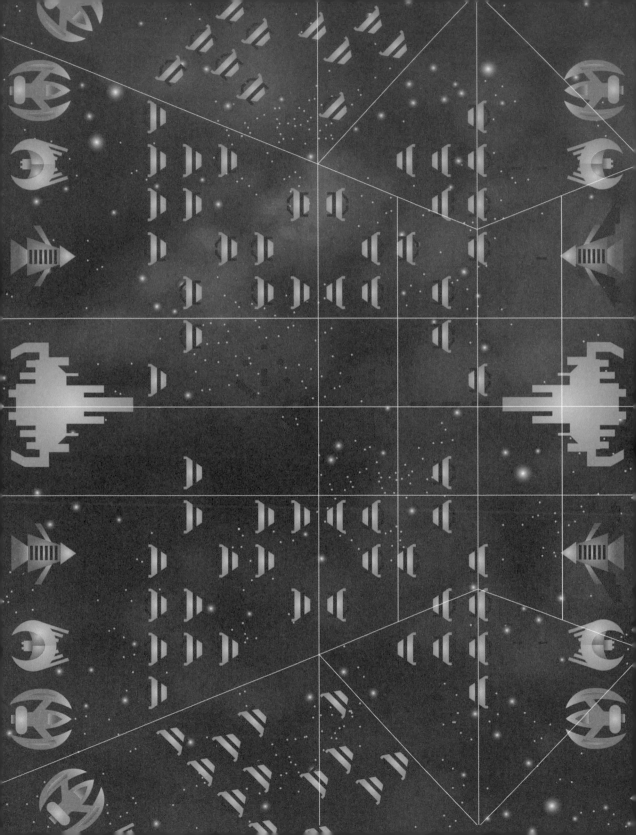

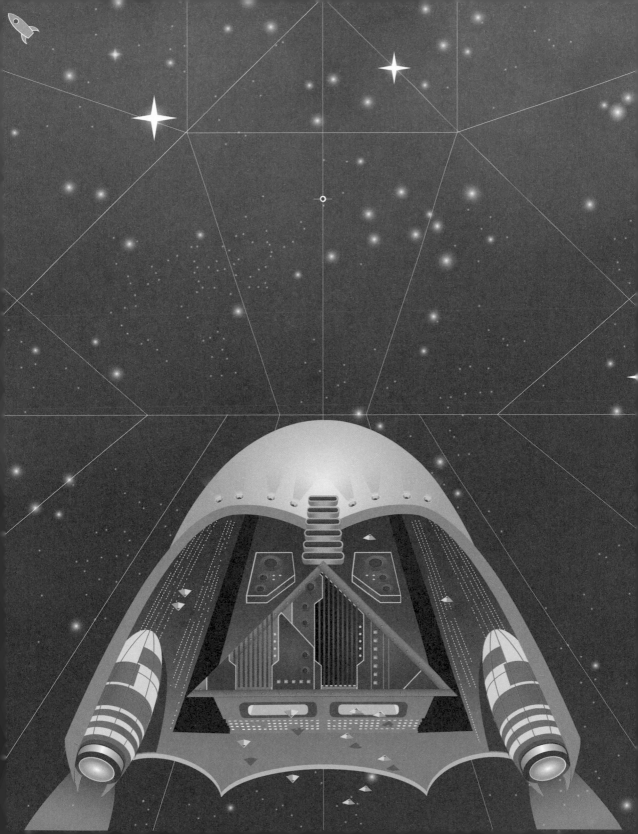

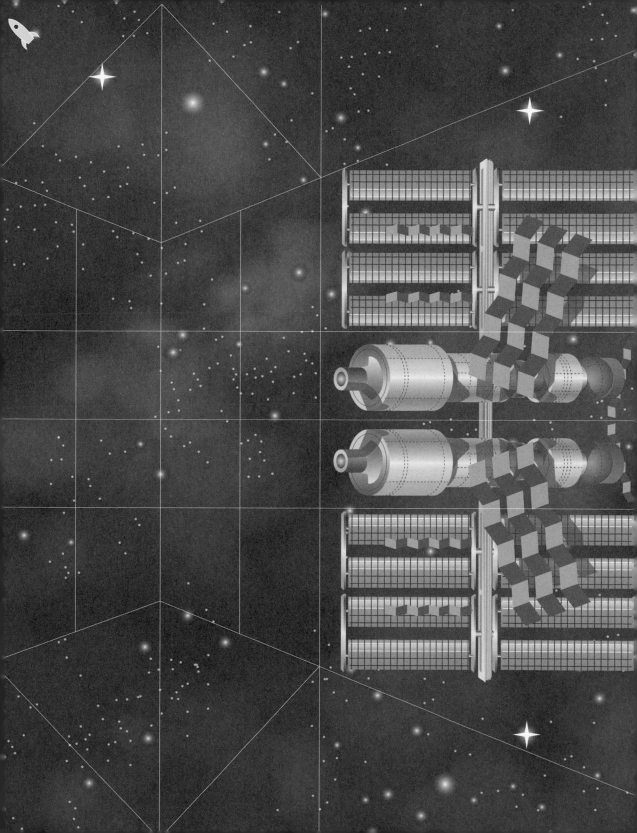

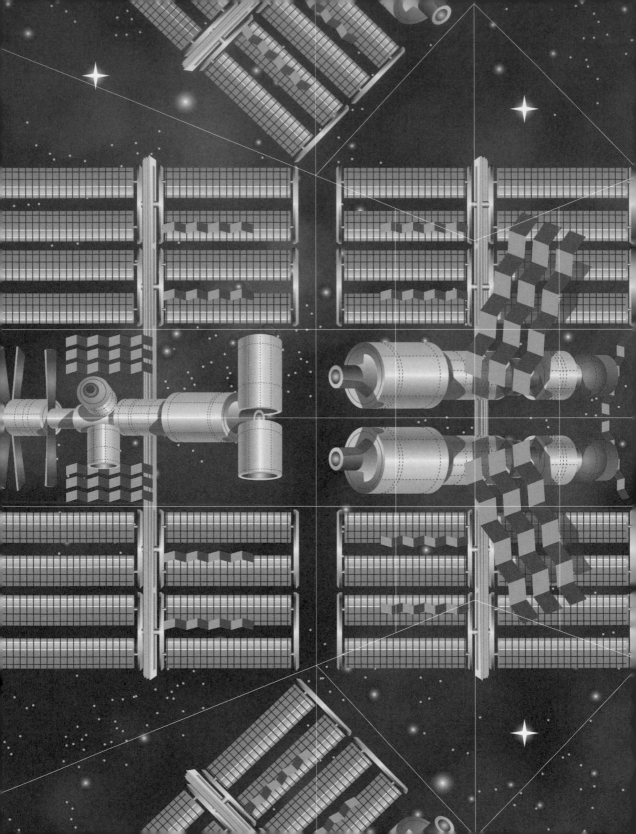

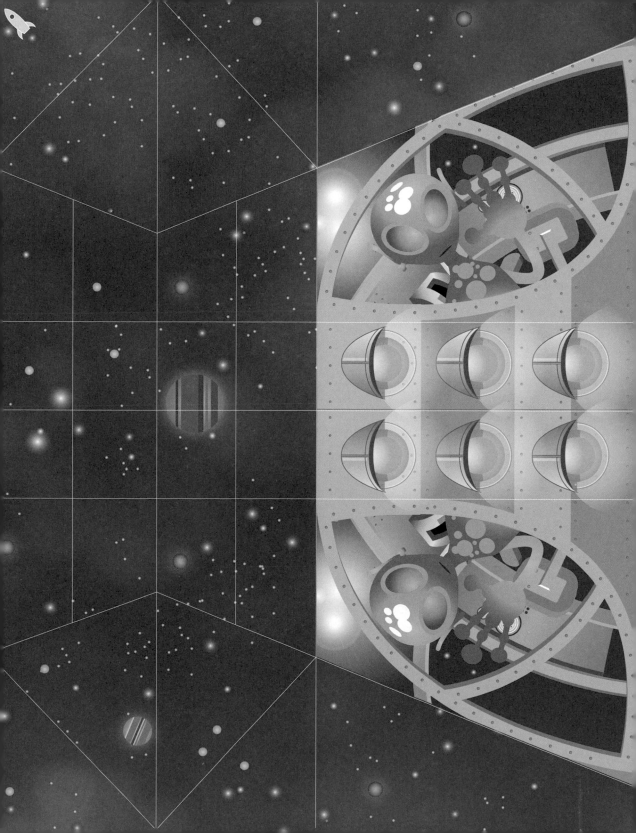

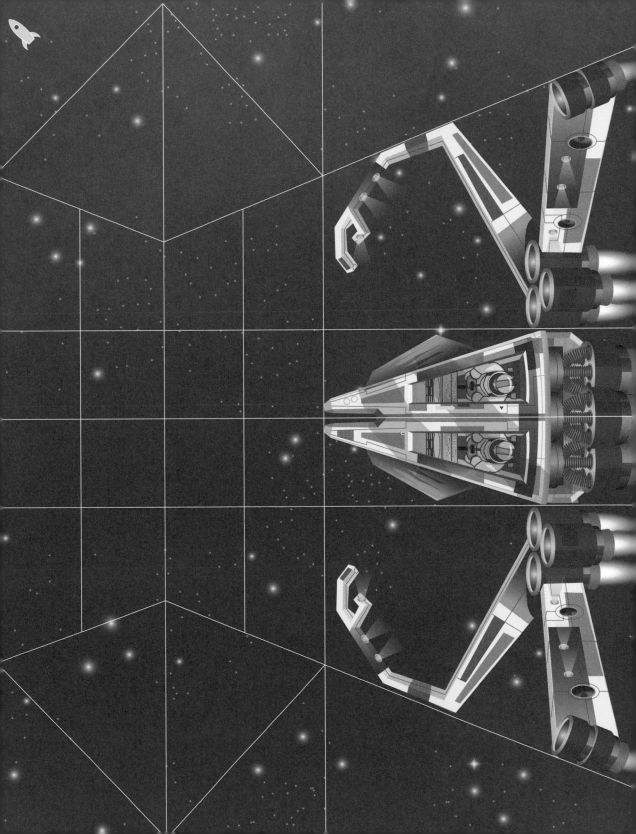

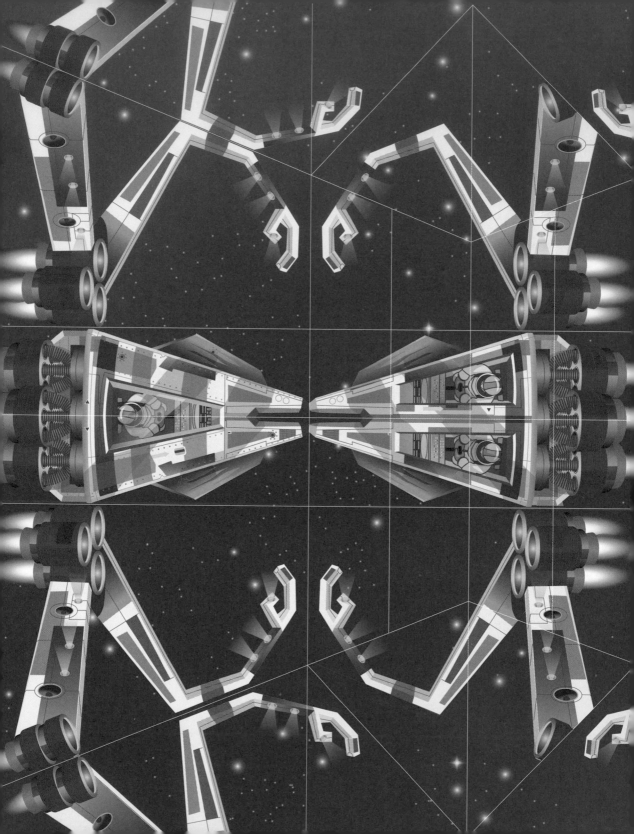

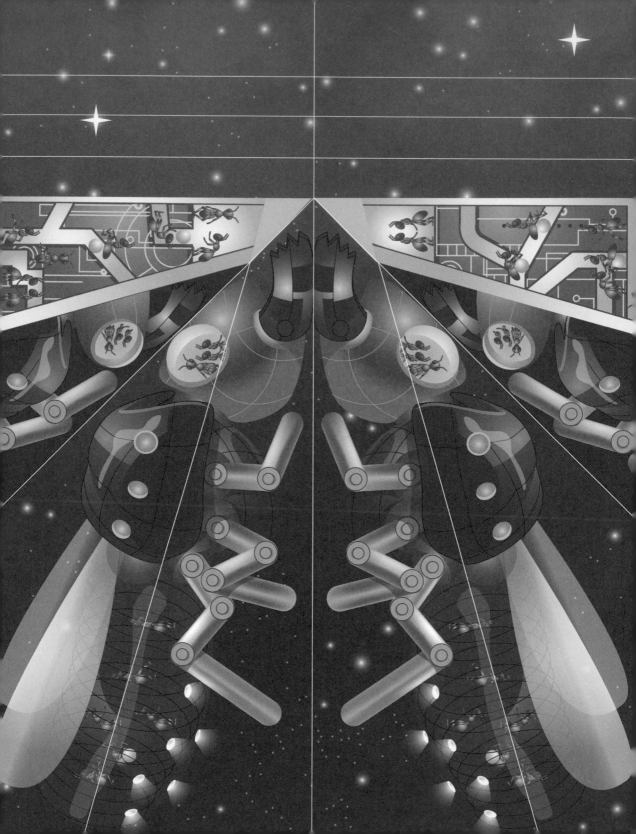

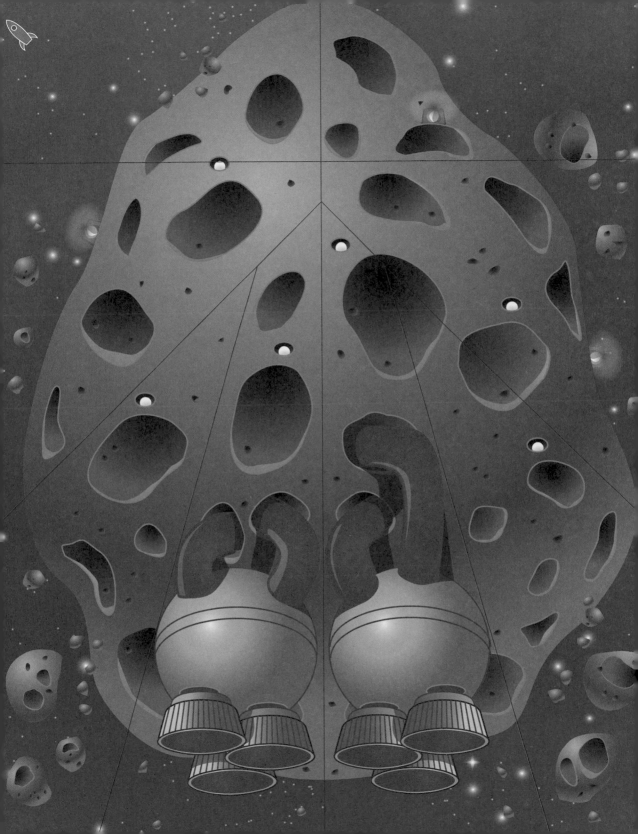

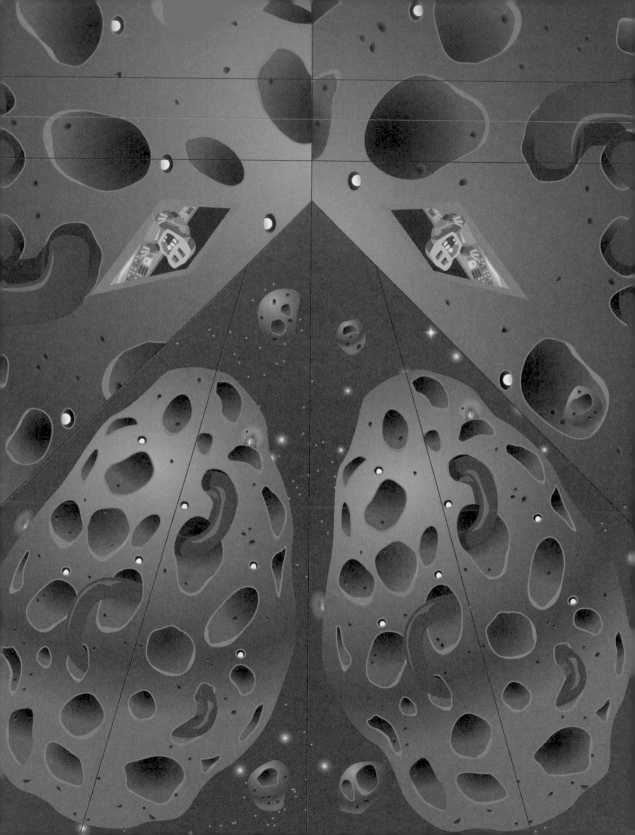

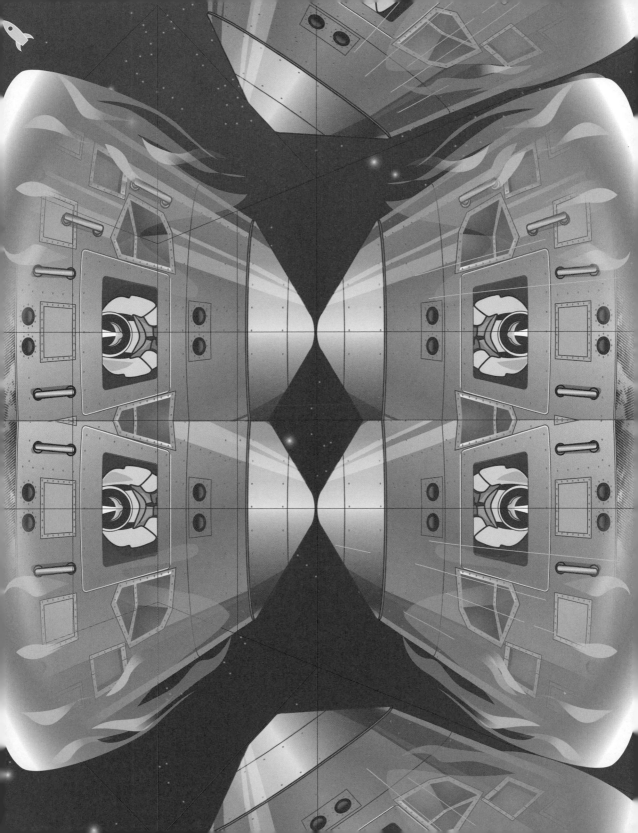

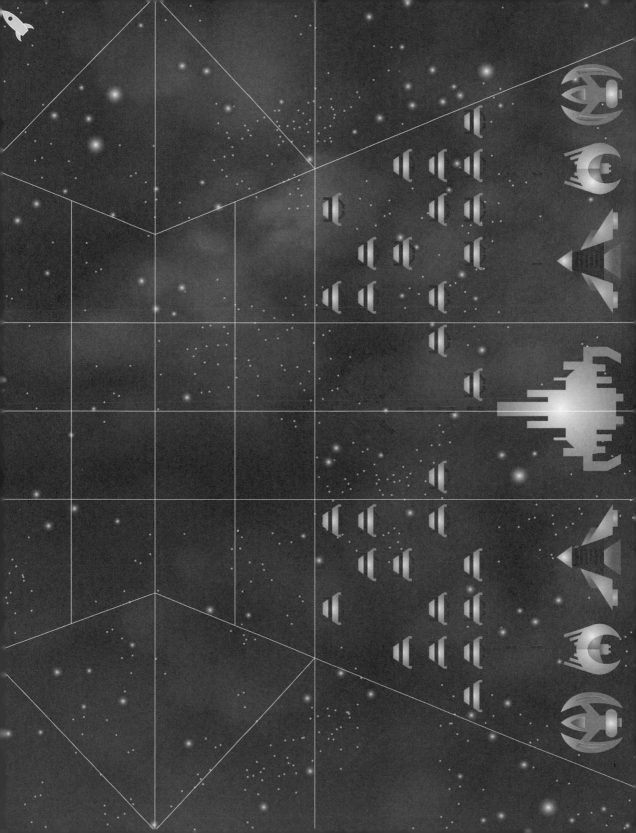

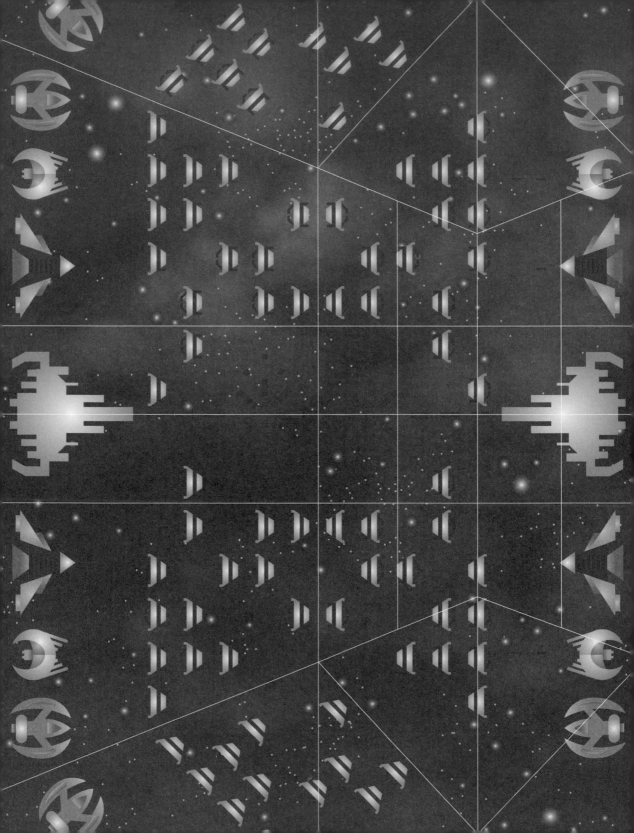

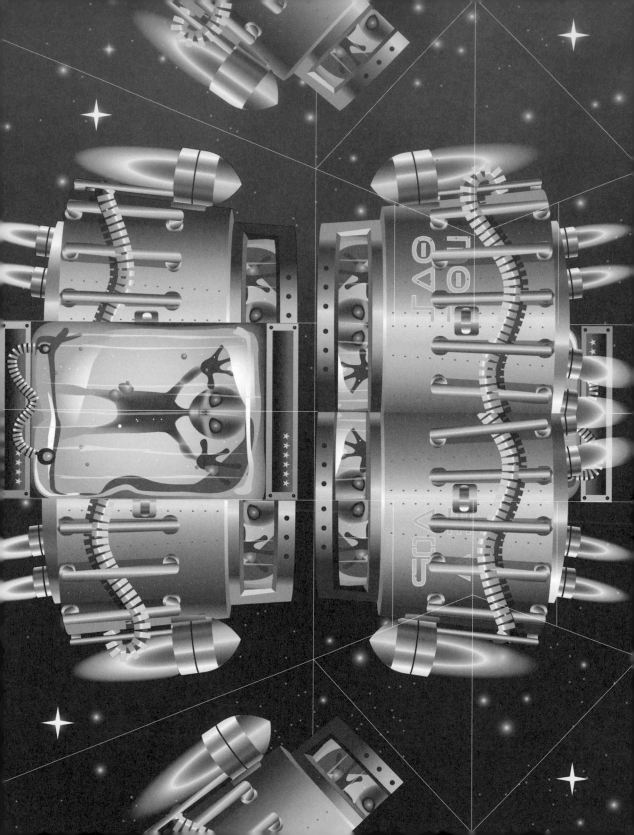

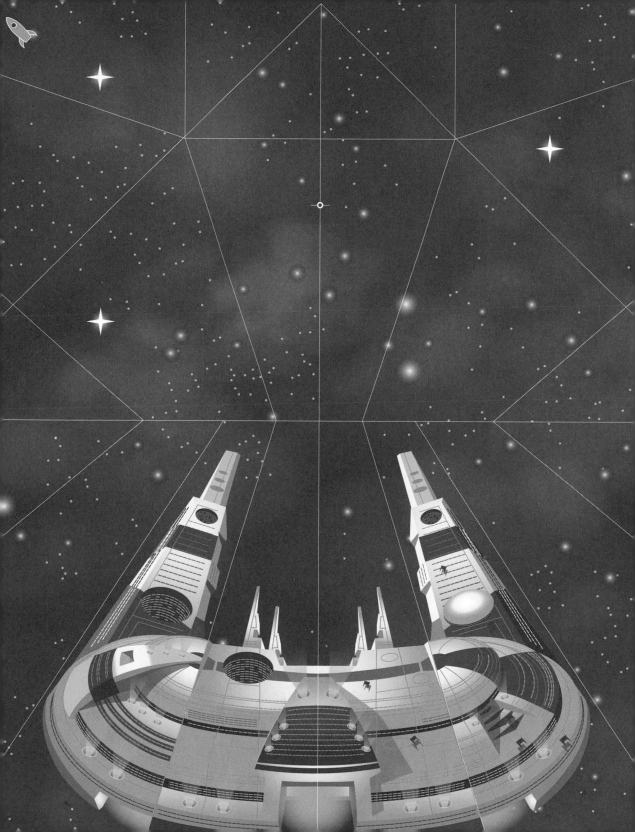

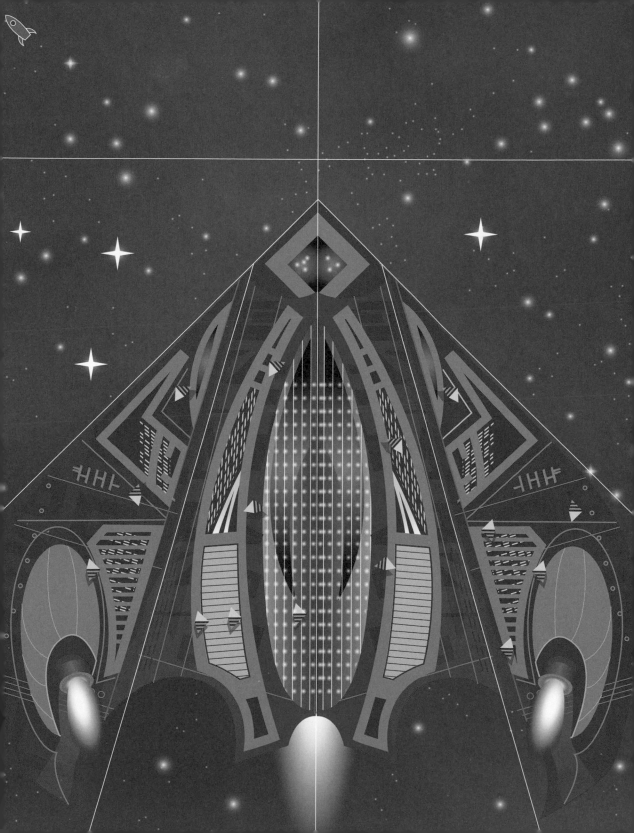

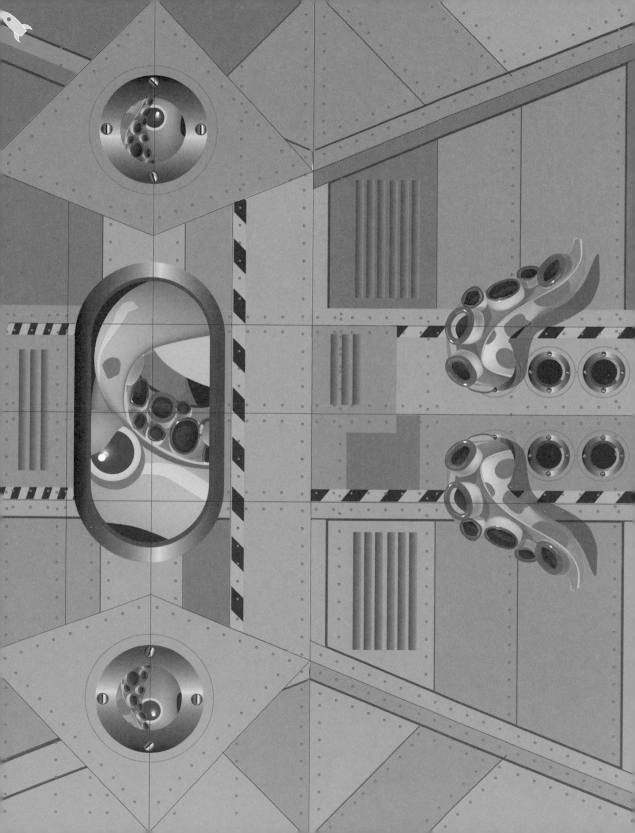

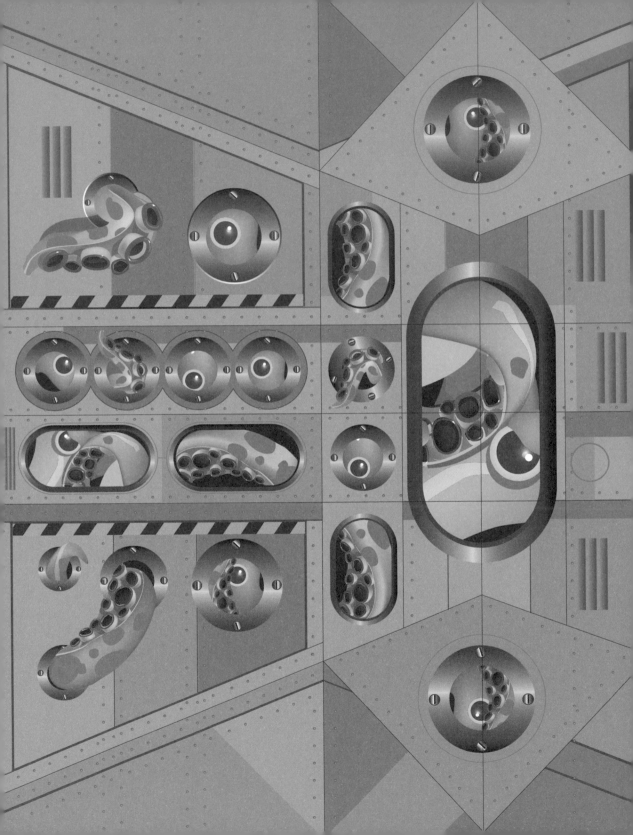

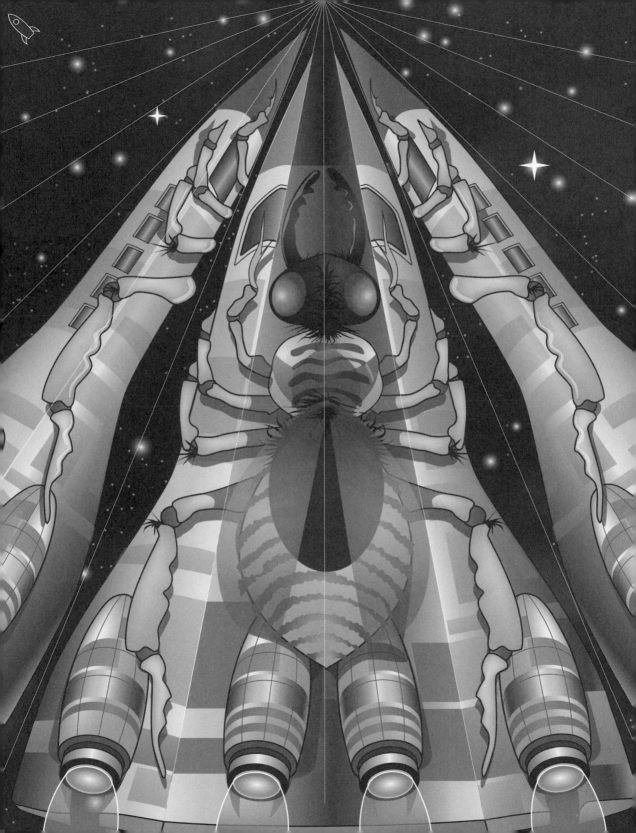

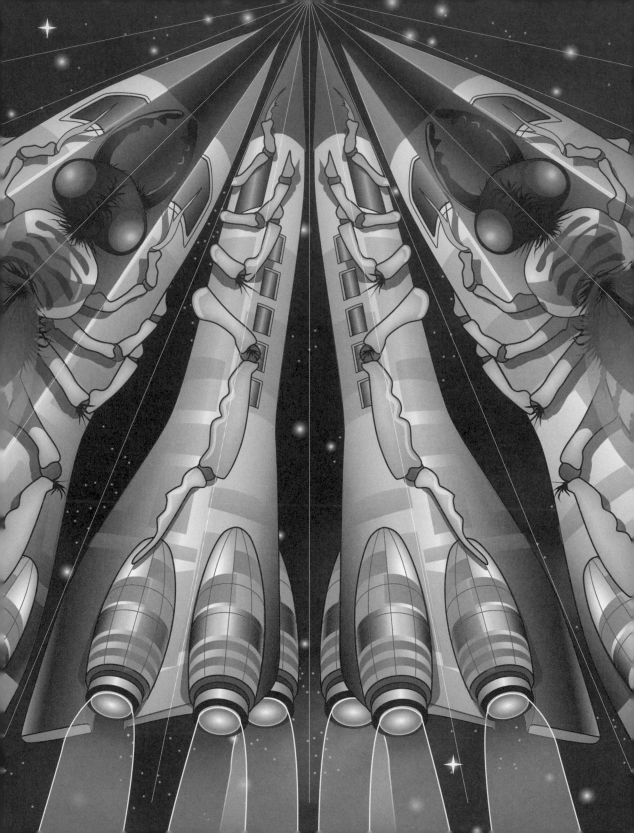

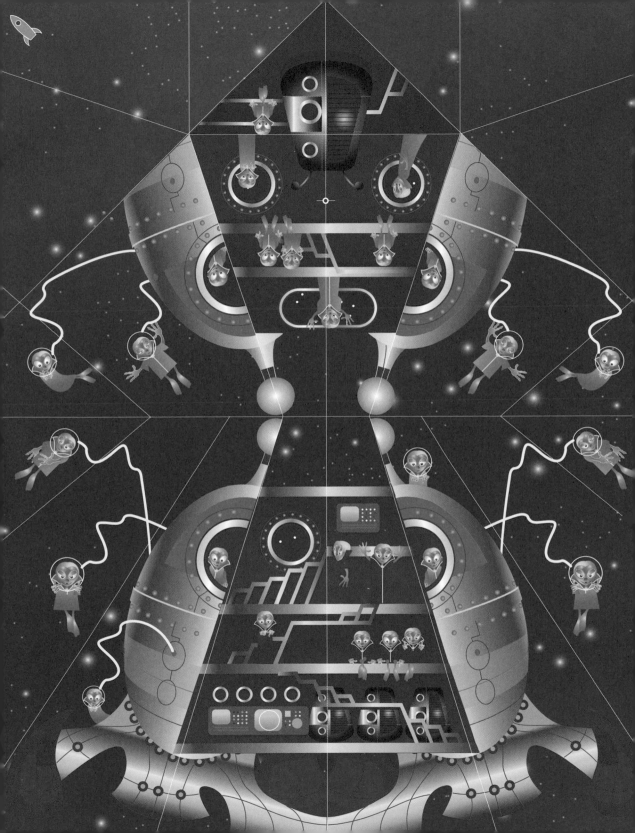

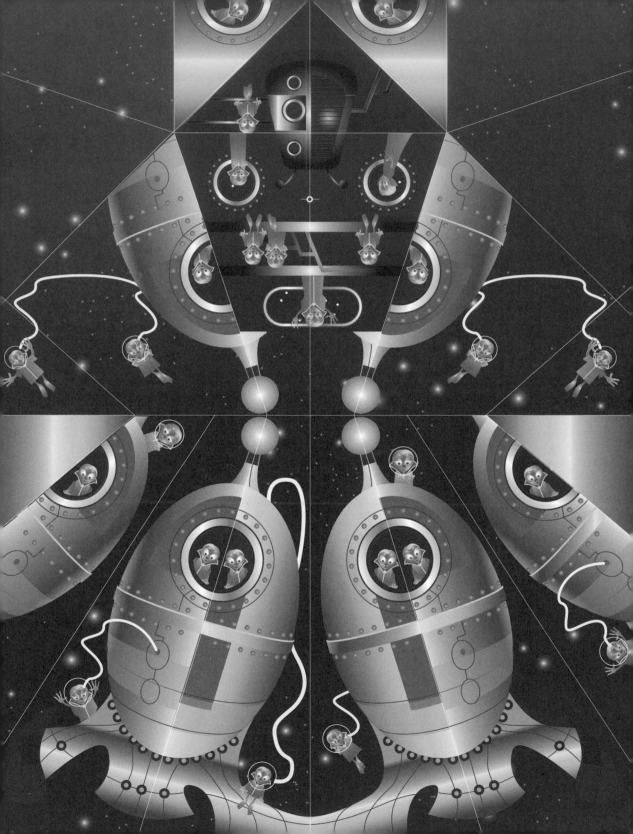

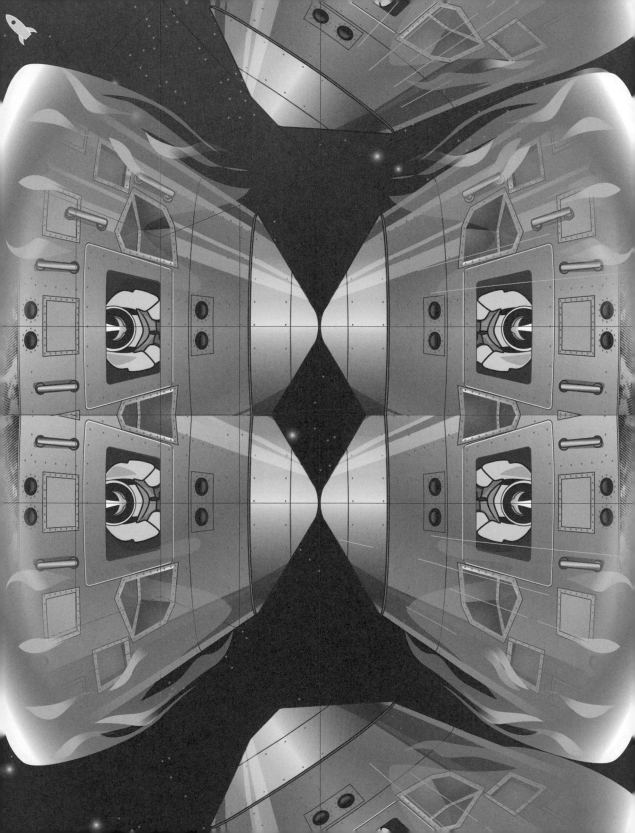

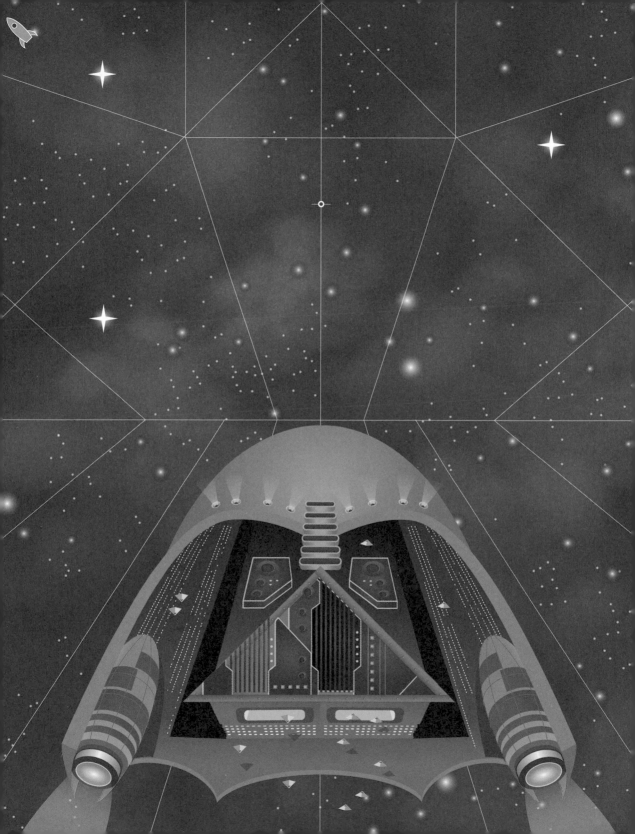

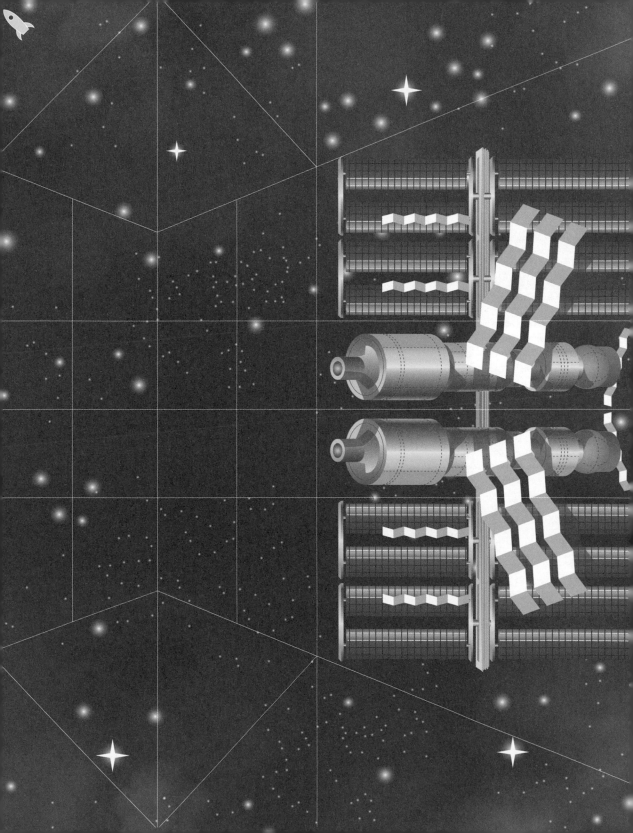

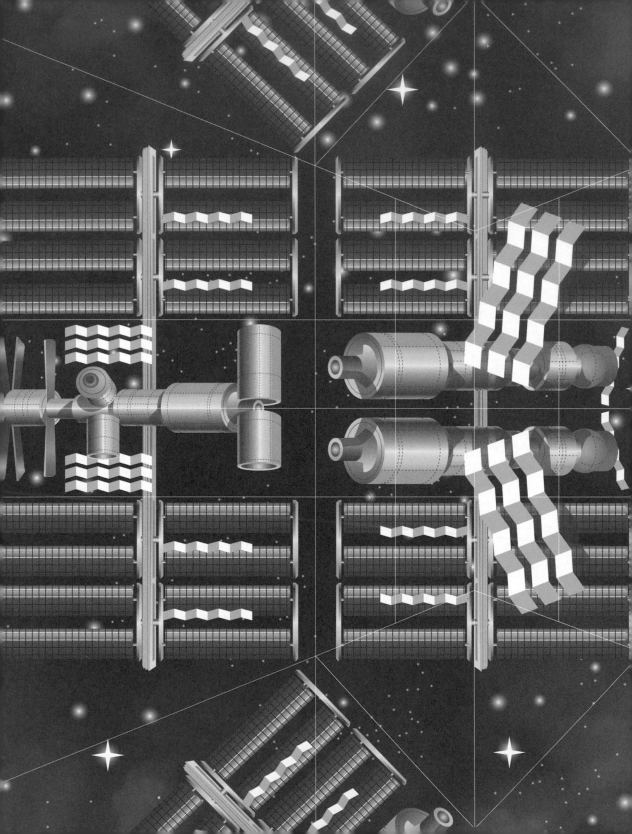

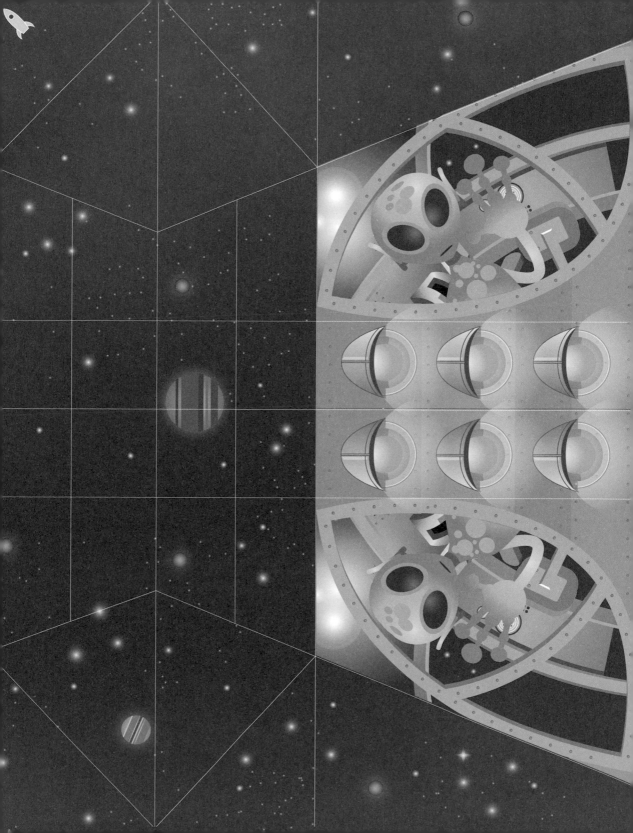

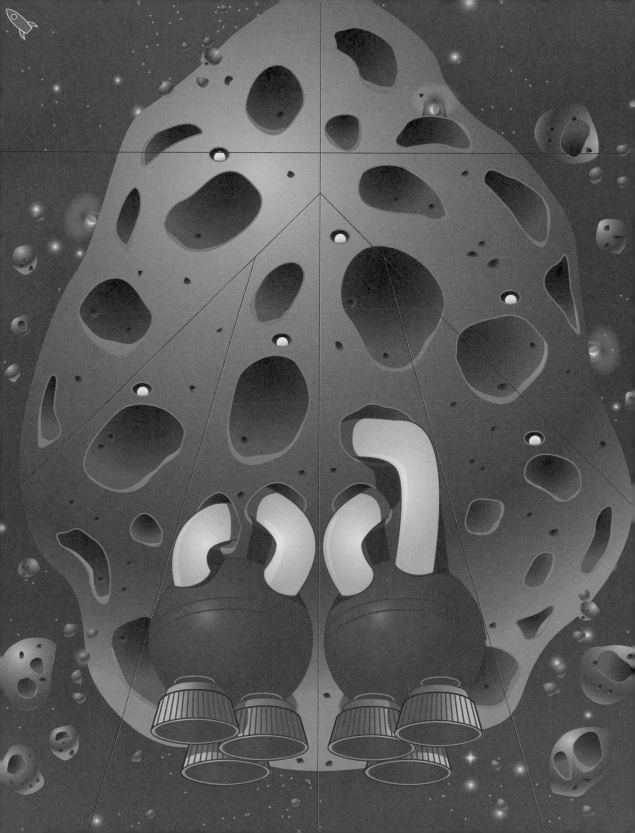

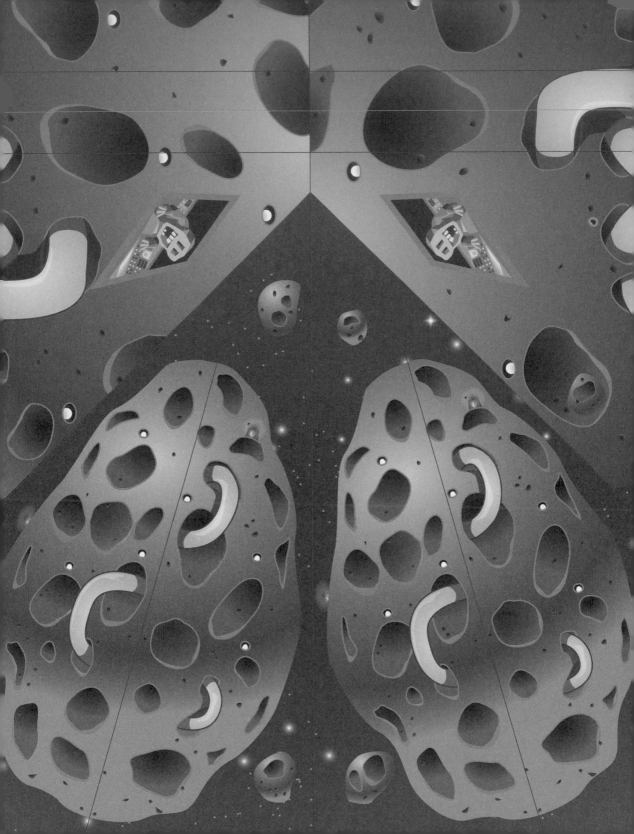

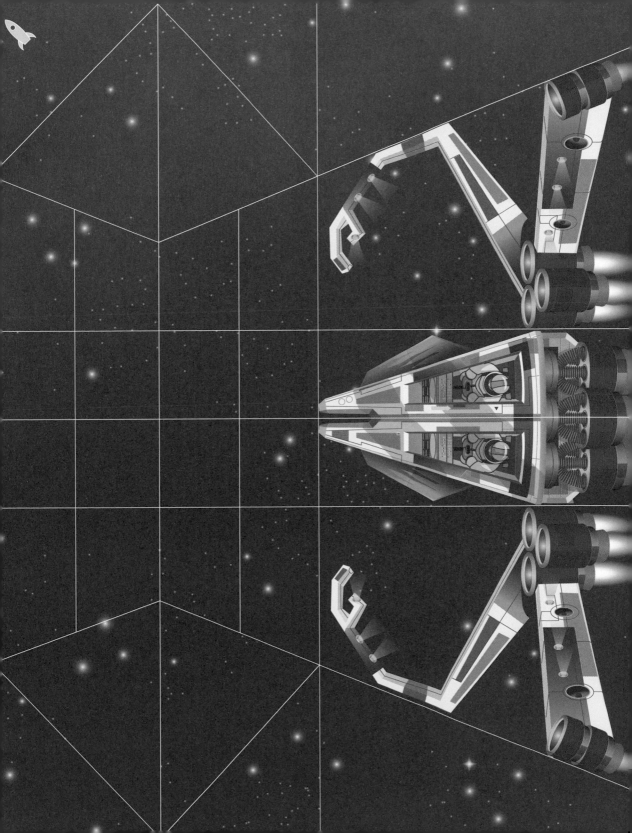

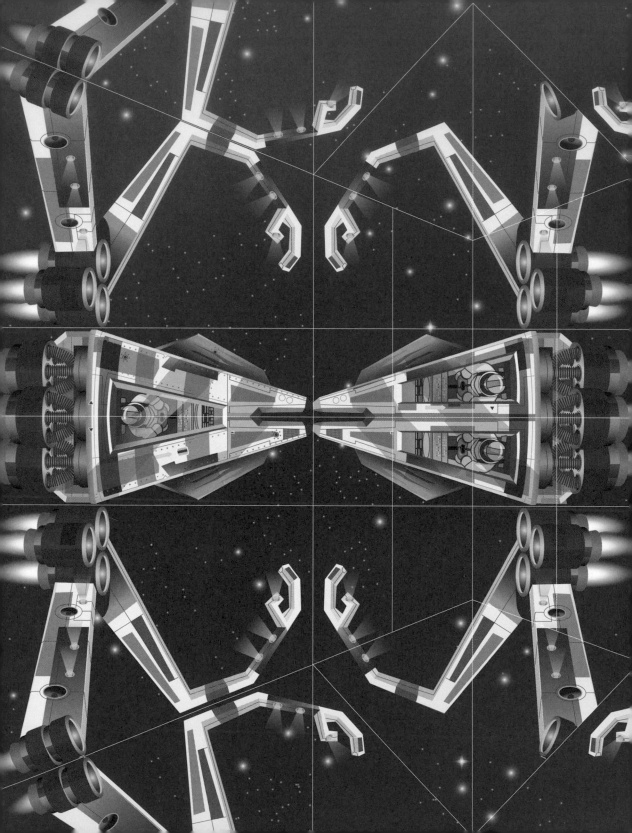

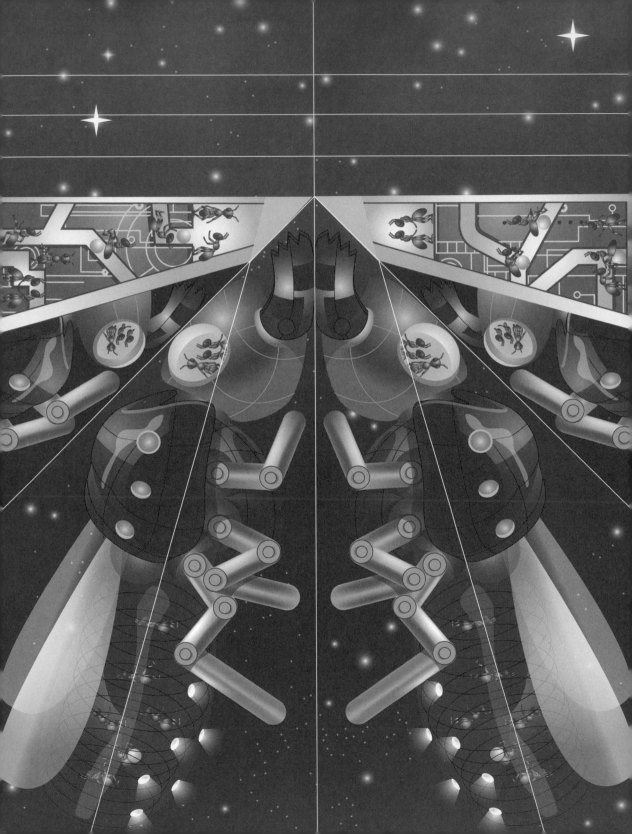